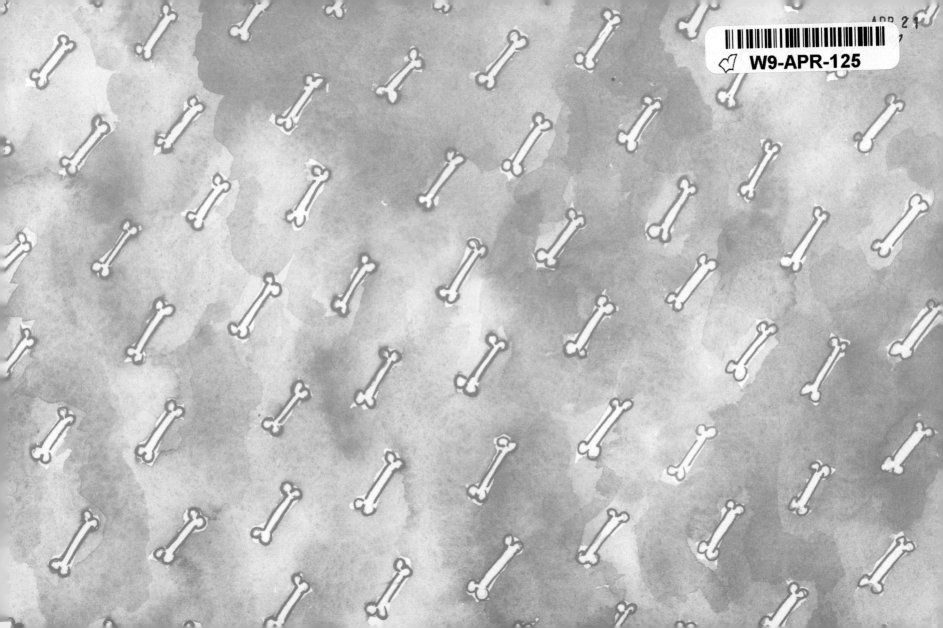

Poojo's Got Wheels

Poojo's Got Wheels

by Charrow

This is Poojo.

He was born without back legs.

But he's got wheels.

He can do anything.

He does fancy tricks.

He's got cool pockets to store stuff.

He's a good friend to everyone . . . .

and everything.

He is fast and clever.

Poojo got a flat.

Good thing Poojo is also extremely creative.

Too big.

Too small.

Definitely too dangerous.

What a good dog you are!

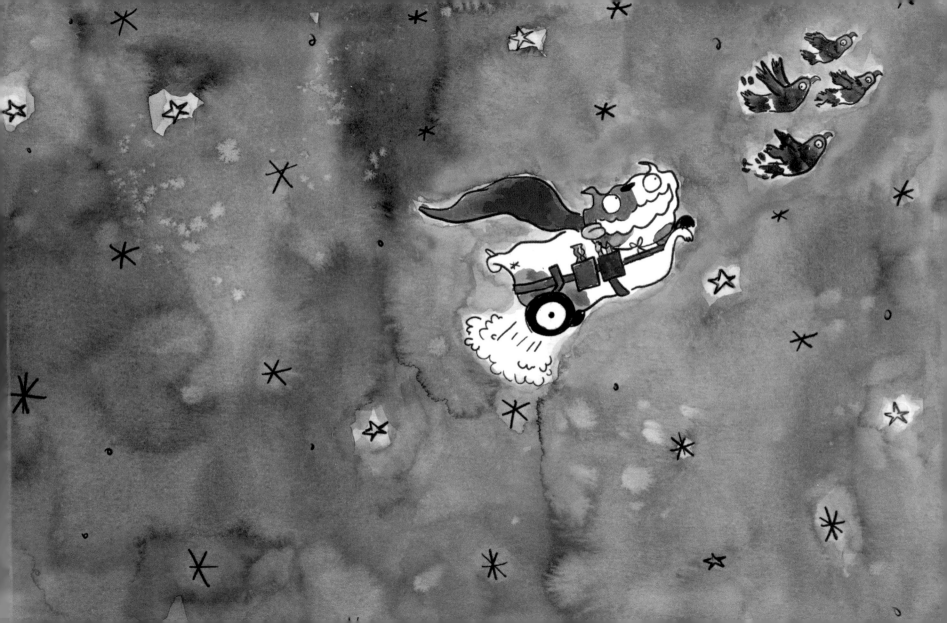

To my mom, who believed in me even when
I couldn't see the way forward

First edition 2021

Library of Congress Catalog Card Number pending
ISBN 978-1-5362-1036-1

20 21 22 23 24 25 APS 10 9 8 7 6 5 4 3 2 1

Printed in Humen, Dongguan, China

This book was typeset in Sariah.
The illustrations were created digitally and with gouache.

Candlewick Press
99 Dover Street
Somerville, Massachusetts 02144

www.candlewick.com

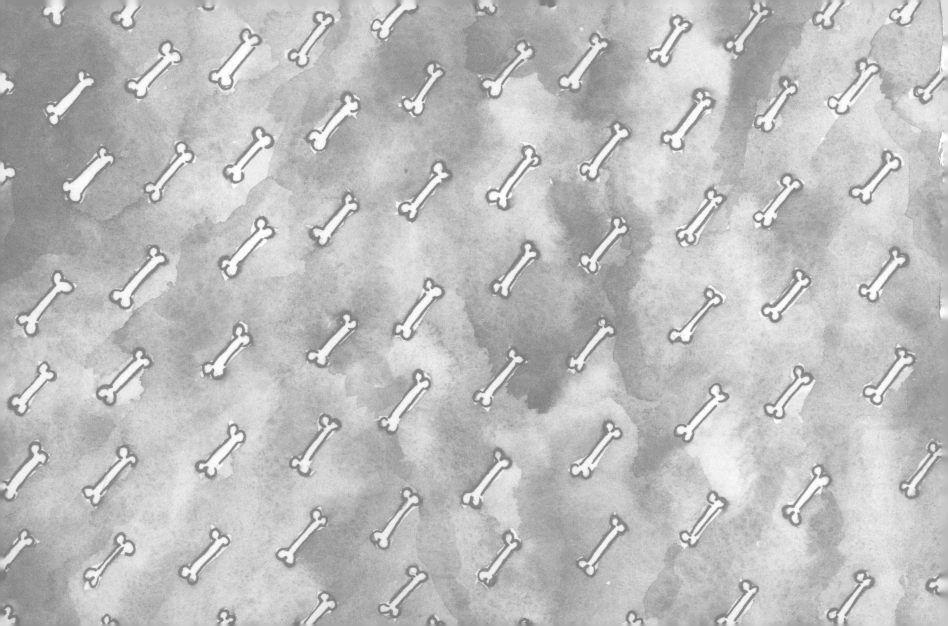

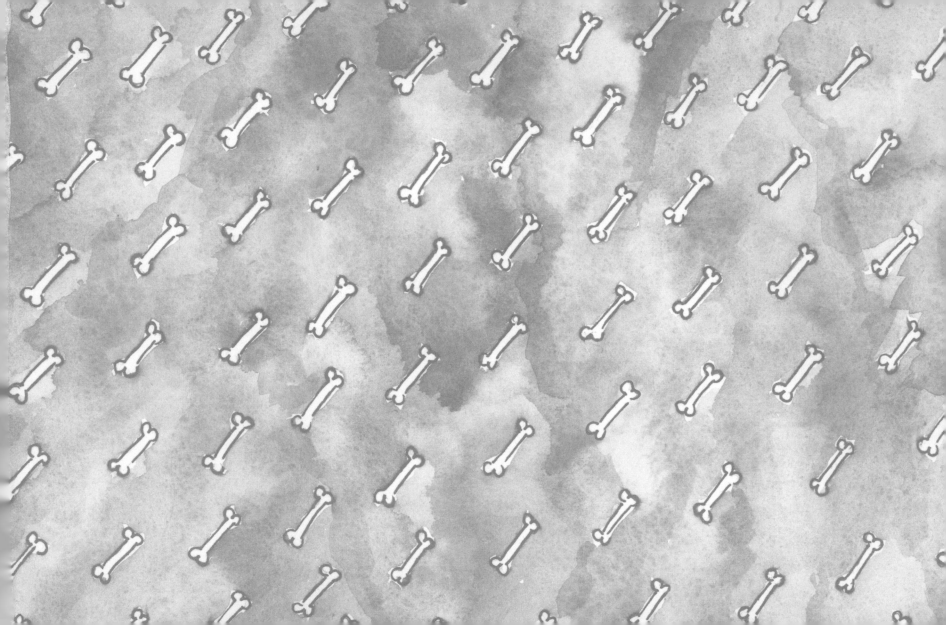